This Puffin Book

belongs to

T0342580

Tick the
Puffin Nibbles
you have read!

☐ **BAD BUSTER**
Sofie Laguna
Illustrated by Leigh Hobbs

☐ **BLAST OFF!**
Margaret Clark
Illustrated by Tom Jellett

☐ **FAIRY BREAD**
Ursula Dubosarsky
Illustrated by Mitch Vane

☐ **SCRUFFY'S DAY OUT**
Rachel Flynn
Illustrated by Jocelyn Bell

☐ **THE LITTLEST PIRATE**
Sherryl Clark
Illustrated by Tom Jellett

☐ **THE MERMAID'S TAIL**
Raewyn Caisley
Illustrated by Ann James

Visit us at puffin.com.au

Puffin Nibbles

Scruffy's Day Out

Rachel Flynn
Illustrated by **Jocelyn Bell**

Puffin Books

PUFFIN BOOKS

UK | USA | Canada | Ireland | Australia
India | New Zealand | South Africa | China

Penguin
Random House
Australia

Penguin Random House Australia is part of the Penguin Random House group of
companies whose addresses can be found at global.penguinrandomhouse.com.

First published by Penguin Books Australia in 2001
This edition published by Puffin Books, an imprint of
Penguin Random House Australia Pty Ltd, in 2019

Design by Lynn Twelftree and Tony Palmer
© Penguin Random House Australia Pty Ltd
Typeset in New Century School Book by
Post Pre-press Group, Brisbane, Queensland

Printed and bound in Australia by Griffin Press, an accredited
ISO AS/NZS 14001 Environmental Management Systems printer

A catalogue record for this
book is available from the
National Library of Australia

ISBN 978 0 14 131169 2. (Paperback)

penguin.com.au

For Devin, who really did
rescue a little scruffy dog
from in front of a truck. *R.F.*

To Edward and Richard
for their care and training
of our dog Bonnie. *J.B.*

1
The Jones Boys

There are five boys in our family.

Jesse (3) wants a dog.

Joel (6) collects sticks.

Me, Justin (almost 9).

John (12) loves cricket.

And Jack (17) who loves
Kristy Madison from his
maths class.

See how all our names
start with 'J'? Mum only
makes one set of name
tags for our school things.

They all say 'J. Jones'
because Jones is our last
name. We are the Jones
boys.

Mum says she really has
six boys because she is
counting Dad as one.

That's because he likes to
play a lot. He plays cricket
in the driveway, footy in
the backyard and frisbee
in the park.

He also likes to fix the
car on the weekend. It's
an old white Valiant with
different-coloured doors and
a purple tailgate.

Last Sunday Dad was
fixing the Valiant when
he suddenly dashed onto

the road in front of a Land
Rover. It was old and dirty
with a rusty bull bar.

We were playing cricket
in the driveway.

I was batting, so I saw
what happened.

Jack (17) was bowling.
He had his back to the road
and didn't see a thing.

John (12) was fielding at silly mid-on, so he didn't see anything either.

Jesse (3) won't play cricket because he hates getting out. He was rolling in the leaves so he only saw the wide blue sky.

But Joel (6) was wicket keeper. He saw everything. He said, 'Cripes, Dad! That was close.'

Mum was on the porch

with our baby sister Shelly.

Mum said, 'Aaaaahhhh!!'

and Shelly said, 'Mmmmm.'

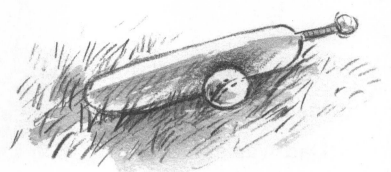

2
Whose Dog?

Dad didn't get killed by the
Land Rover. He rolled out
of the way just in time.

When he came back into
the yard, he had a little
scruffy dog in his arms.

He put it on the ground and it stood there shaking.

Dad was shaking too because of seeing the rusty bull bar up really close and nearly getting squashed.

Jesse (3) came over to stare at the dog.

Joel (6) stopped being wicket keeper and said, 'Dad, did you see what that was? It was an army truck with a tarp over the back.

I got its number. IBP S17.'

John (12) stayed at silly mid-on and said, 'Come on, guys. We can't stop in the middle of an over.'

Jack (17) threw the ball up and down in the air and said, 'Good work, Dad. You saved the dog's life. Does that mean we can keep it?'

'It must belong to someone,' said Dad.

Shelly pointed at the dog and said, 'Mmmmm.'

'Lunch is ready,' said Mum.

So we all went inside.
Mum gave the dog a
weetbix soaked in warm
water. It ate it in twenty-
three seconds and licked the
bowl all around the kitchen.

Then it sat on the floor in front of Mum and banged its tail on the tiles.

Mum looked at Dad and said, 'It's a lovely dog, but we can't keep it.'

Dad took his hat off and scratched his head. Then he went out to the shed and got some tattered old rope.

'Righto, you boys,' he said, as he tied the rope around the dog's neck.

'You can take the scruffy dog for a walk and see who owns him. Knock on a few doors. Someone will recognise him.'

The dog stood up ready to go and licked Dad's hand.

'Who wants to hold the lead?' asked Dad.

'Me,' said Jesse. He grabbed the rope from Dad.

'In that case, Jack,' said Mum, 'you'll have to hold

Jesse's hand so he doesn't
run on the road.'

'And I'll go,' said Joel,
'because I need some more
sticks.'

'You can all go,' said Dad.

'But what about the cricket?' said John. 'We're in the middle of an over.'

We all went.

Jack (17) held hands with Jesse (3), who was holding the lead. The scruffy dog stopped to sniff at things all the time.

John (12) and I (almost 9) had to watch that Joel (6) didn't have any accidents or collect too many sticks.

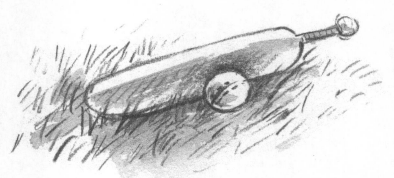

3
Cake, Cricket, Maths, Sticks

Lots of people were outside so we didn't have to knock on many doors.

First we saw a whole family having a picnic in their garden.

'Do you recognise this
dog?' John yelled at them.

A lady came over to the
fence. 'No, I don't know that
dog,' she said. 'Is he lost?'

'Our dad rescued him
from in front of an army
truck,' Joel told her. 'He
rolled out of the way just
in time.'

Everybody looked at the
dog. He sat on the path and
pricked up his ears.

'You're such good boys
to take him around,' said
the lady, and she gave each
of us a piece of cake on a
yellow serviette.

Next we found a tall girl
and a small boy playing on
the nature strip.

'Do you recognise this
dog?' John asked them.

They looked at the dog
carefully.

'He's very scruffy,' said
the girl. 'Did you find him?'

The dog sniffed at them
both, then waved his tail
hopefully.

'Our dad rescued him

from in front of a rusty old truck,' Joel told her. 'They could have been *killed!*'

'He looks pretty happy
with you,' said the boy.
'Maybe you should keep him.'

Later we came to a house
that had its front door right
on the footpath. We could
hear the television.

'It's the cricket,' said John.
'Come on, we'll find out the
score.'

He knocked on the door
and after a while an old
man came out.

'Do you recognise this
dog?' John asked him.

'It's a little Maltese cross,'
said the man. 'He's a bit
scruffy – needs a bath and
a trim.'

The dog ate something it
found in the grass.

'Our dad saved his life from in front of a speeding truck,' Joel told him. 'They both *nearly died!*'

Suddenly a huge cheer came from the television.

'What's the score?' asked John.

The old man shuffled back inside.

'That's three out for thirty-three,' he yelled out to us.

The next door we knocked

on was blue with red panes
of glass.

'Coming,' someone yelled.
The door opened and
there stood Kristy Madison
from Jack's maths class.

They stared at each other
for minutes. Then John
interrupted.

'Do you recognise this
dog?' he asked.

Kristy looked at the dog.

'He is so cute,' she said as she patted him. 'Are these all your brothers, Jack?'

Jack was speechless so I had to help him out.

'This is John,' I said.

'He's twelve. I'm Justin, almost nine. This is Joel, six. And this is Jesse. He's three. We're taking this dog around to see who owns him.'

'Our dad rescued him off the road from in front of a runaway army truck,' Joel told her. 'It was totally out of control. They could have both been *killed stone dead*.'

Kristy looked shocked.

'He is so cute,' she said
again, kneeling down to pat
the dog.

The dog licked her hand
and wagged his tail.

Then Kristy smiled up
at Jack. 'That maths
homework is so hard,' she
said. 'Maybe we should do
it together.'

They looked at each other
for ages without talking.
At last Jack said, 'I'll just

go home and get my books.'

'See you later then,' said Kristy, and she closed the door.

'Right, come on,' said Jack. 'We're going home now. Hey, where's Joel?'

I had to run and get Joel
from way down the road
where he was collecting
sticks.

So then we went home.

Jack (17) pulled Jesse (3), who dragged the scruffy dog, which stopped to smell things all the time. John (12) ran ahead so he could get home quickly to watch the cricket. I walked behind to mind Joel (6), who had collected two sticks and a long leafy branch.

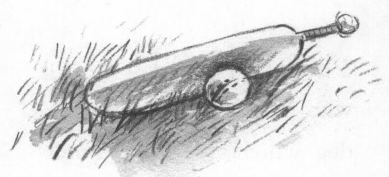

4
Lost and Found

When we got home Dad was
polishing the Valiant with
some old jocks. Mum was
sitting in the sun reading
the paper and Shelly was
crawling in the leaves.

John rushed inside to
watch the cricket.

Jack rushed inside to get
his maths books.

Joel showed his long leafy
branch to Mum and Dad.

Jesse let go of the rope
and rolled in the leaves
with Shelly.

The dog lay down in the
sun at Mum's feet, yawned
and went to sleep.

Then Jack rushed out again and said, 'Got to go. See ya.'

'You brought the dog home then,' said Dad.

'No one knew whose it was,' I explained.

'The family who lost the dog might have phoned the RSPCA,' said Mum.

'Really?' I said. 'So we could call them and see.'

I went inside and looked

up their number, then brought the phone out to Mum.

'You do it,' she said, so I did. I dialled the number – 9224 2222. First I got a recorded message. It said to press '2' for lost and found

pets. Then a real person answered.

She wanted to know what sort of dog it was.

'It's a small, scruffy dog,' I said. Then I remembered the old man watching the cricket. 'It's a cross Maltese.'

She said someone had called about a lost dog, so she gave me their phone number.

'Go on, you ring them,'
said Mum.

I dialled their number.
It rang for a long time.
I thought no one was going
to answer it. Mum was
listening with me. Dad was
leaning on the car watching
us. Jesse and Shelly were
still playing in the leaves,
and Joel was sorting out his
sticks

Suddenly the phone

stopped ringing and a man
answered, 'Yep?'

'I think we've found your
dog,' I said.

I heard him yelling in
the background, 'Someone's
found the dog.'

'What's it look like?' he
asked.

'Small and scruffy,' I said,
'a cross Maltese.'

'Maltese cross. Yep, that'd
be him. Where do you live?'

So I told him and he said
he'd be straight over.

Their car was an old
Valiant just like ours, only
better. When they pulled
up, Dad said, 'Look at the
paintwork on that.'

A father and a girl got
out.

The father said g'day
and started to chat to Dad
about Valiants.

The girl rushed up to the
dog and cuddled it. 'Scruffy,'
she said, 'you're found.'

The dog licked her face
and waved his tail.

Jesse stopped rolling in
the leaves to come and stare.

Joel dragged his branch
over to show her.

John came out of the
house to see whose dog it
was.

'Is he really your dog?'
asked Jesse.

The girl nodded.

'Is his name really
Scruffy?' asked John.

The girl nodded again.

'Our dad rescued him
from in front of an out-
of- control, speeding army
truck,' Joel told her. 'They
almost both got *killed
dead!*'

The girl just looked at us
all, so I thought I'd better do
a proper introduction

'This is Jesse,' I started.
'He's three. And this is Joel,
six. I'm Justin, almost nine.
And this is John, twelve.'

Shelly had crawled up to
us and tried to climb my leg,
so I picked her up. 'And this
is our baby sister Shelly,'
I added. 'She's not even one
yet.'

Shelly pointed to the girl
and said, 'Mmmm-mm-uu.'

'I'm Monica,' said the girl.
'I'm almost nine too. We
just shifted in and Scruffy

can get under the gate. Dad
has to fix it.'

'Where do you live?' I
asked.

'Round that street,'
she pointed, 'then round
another street and another
street I think. I don't know
anyone yet.'

'You know us,' said Joel.

'S'pose so.'

'Are you sure he's your
dog?' asked Jesse.

'Yep, because he's got
a spot, see, just here.'
'Can you play cricket?'
asked John.
'Yep.'

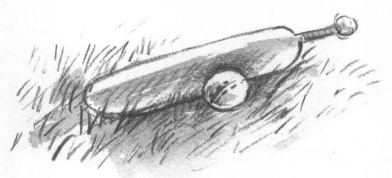

5
Not Out

'Come on then,' said John.
'It was the middle of an
over, right? There were four
balls to go. You were
batting, Justin. You were
keeping wicket, Joel. I was

fielding, and Jack was bowling. Oh no, Jack's gone. What are we going to do?'

'I can bowl,' said Monica. And so she did.

I hit the ball over her head, over the fence and onto the road.

I should have got six, except that Scruffy chased the ball down the driveway and under the gate.

We all saw the truck this
time. It was a supermarket
delivery truck and was
totally out of control.

The ten-tonne truck and
the little scruffy dog were
going to collide!

'*SCRUFFY*' we all yelled at exactly the same time.

Scruffy skidded and turned to look at us.

He pricked up his ears
and wagged his tail.

'*Ruff?*' he said, just like
he was saying, *What? What
do you want?*

The truck rushed straight
past and just missed him.

Just missed him by that
much!

That much!

'Cripes,' said Joel. 'That
was close.'

Monica ran down the

drive and grabbed Scruffy,
and John ran onto the road
and picked up his ball.

'Oh no,' he said. 'Look,
guys, it's squashed flat.'

Then Monica's father
said, 'Come on, love, better

get that dog home before
he causes any more trouble.
He's already had a big day
out.'

'Thanks for looking after
Scruffy,' said Monica.

They got into their
Valiant and waved as they
roared off up the street.

Dad had finished polishing
the car and put the old
jocks in his back pocket.

'How's that?' he said.

We all looked at the
Valiant. It gleamed and
sparkled white in the
sun, except for the purple

tailgate and the pink and green doors.

'Lovely!' said Mum.

Then Dad got a tennis ball out of the glove box and said, 'I'll bowl. What about you, Jesse? Do you want to play? You can field from over there in the leaves. Shelly, do you want to play?'

Shelly shook her head and pointed to Mum and said, 'Mm-uuumm.'

'Did you hear that?' Mum said to us all. 'Did you hear her say "Mum"? Isn't she a lovely girl! And so clever!'

So we all played cricket –
Jesse (3), Joel (6), me
(almost 9), John (12) and
Dad (41).

Dad bowled me out
straight away, then Jesse
went in to bat. We couldn't
get him out at all because
every time we did, Mum
said, 'Not out.'

From Rachel Flynn

One day my son's friend Devin
arrived at our place with a little
scruffy dog he had rescued. He
rang up all his friends and they
came over to see the dog. Then they
walked around the streets to see
who owned it. Finally they rang
the RSPCA.

I remember this day because the
cricket was on television.

From Jocelyn Bell

I have always had dogs, and lots of other pets too – cats, guinea pigs, rabbits, horses, even white mice.

Every morning I take my big dog for a walk, and a little Maltese-cross, just like Scruffy, always rushes up and barks at us. My dog Bonnie ignores him, but I don't. I've drawn him for this book.

Want another nibble?

Being bad was what Buster
did best. Until his dad thought
of a way to sort him out.

Will Adam ever achieve his
dream of being an astronaut?

Becky only wants fairy bread at
her party. But there's so much left
over, and she won't throw it out.

Nicholas Nosh is the littlest pirate
in the world. He's not allowed to go
to sea, and he's bored. Very bored.
'I'll show them,' he says.

The Mermaid's Tail

Raewyn Caisley

Illustrated by Ann James

Crystal longs to be a mermaid.
So her mother makes her a special
tail. But what will happen when
Crystal wears her tail to bed?

Find your story

puffin.com.au